MARY BLOUNT CHRISTIAN

GOODY SHERMAN'S PIG

ILLUSTRATED BY

DIRK ZIMMER

MACMILLAN PUBLISHING COMPANY   NEW YORK
COLLIER MACMILLAN CANADA   TORONTO

MAXWELL MACMILLAN INTERNATIONAL PUBLISHING GROUP
NEW YORK   OXFORD   SINGAPORE   SYDNEY

Remembering Mother,

who taught me that a great life, like great books,

is made of little chapters

—M.B.C.

First edition   Printed in the United States of America   10   9   8   7   6   5   4   3   2   1

The text of this book is set in 14 point Cheltenham. The illustrations are rendered in pen-and-ink. Library of Congress Cataloging-in-Publication Data · Christian, Mary Blount. Goody Sherman's pig/Mary Blount Christian: illustrated by Dirk Zimmer.   p.   cm. Summary: In Massachusetts in 1636, Goody Sherman begins a legal battle over her pig that ends up dividing the legislative department of the colony into two independent branches. [1. United States—Politics and government—Fiction. 2. Massachusetts—Fiction. 3. Law—Fiction. 4. Pigs—Fiction.] I. Zimmer, Dirk, ill. II. Title.   PZ7.C4528Gd 1991   [E]—dc20   90-35181 CIP AC
ISBN 0-02-718251-7

CONTENTS

GOODY
SHERMAN'S PIG

HEAT rose off Massachusetts Bay in shimmering white waves. Overhead, sea gulls glistened white against the cloudless cornflower blue sky. Their shrill shrieks seemed to protest the banging and clanging that drifted from the shipyard. There men built sailing ships to take lumber and livestock to England and bring tea and gossip back to the New World.

Goody Sherman set down the wooden pails she was carrying and brushed the sweat from her forehead with her sleeve. England. It seemed a lifetime since she'd packed her few clothes, a cooking caldron, and her almanac in a trunk and stood at the stern of the *Arbella,* watching her country fade behind a morning mist.

She'd looked forward to becoming one of the planters, as the king had called them, planting herself in the New World. Coming here had seemed like heaven then.

Some heaven it had turned out to be—six years of knee-numbing winters and mosquito-infested summers, and this summer of 1636 seemed the worst of them. Still, it was no worse than London, with its soot-laden fogs and shoulder-to-shoulder people, she reckoned. She inhaled deeply. At least here a body could breathe, even if the air did bear the odor of salty sea and fish.

Goody dabbed the sweat from her face once more and glanced around her. From the chimneys of the look-alike, whitewashed houses, wisps of gray smoke drifted lazily, carrying the smells of spicy suppers simmering.

She stirred the air with her hand. "It's so hot a body could bake beans out here," she muttered. Sighing, she picked up the pails once more. In one was fresh well water, and in the other were corncobs, carrot tops, and two-day-old bread soaked in broth.

Goody scurried past the rows of houses and down the road a piece. Livestock were kept more than a smell away from the thatch-roofed homes, but on a hot day like this she covered the distance in no more than a hop and two jogs.

Stepping through the gate to her pigpen, Goody called, "Sooey, Piggy Pig pig pig. Victuals here, Piggy Pig."

From a little shed at the back of the pen, a large white sow with a black spot the size of a shilling under her right eye and one ragged ear trotted toward Goody, squealing joyfully. *Ronk ronk wheeeee wheeeeee.*

Piggy Pig was the daughter of Piggy Pig I, who'd traveled in the hold of the *Arbella* when Goody and her husband came to the New World. Goody had traded Piggy Pig I for a cow that first hard winter. And she'd bartered away all her piglets but Piggy Pig, the pick of the litter.

Since then Piggy Pig had rewarded Goody with fine litters that paid the lease on their house lot and the garden plot, with enough left over for a few niceties, too, like molasses and spices, a sugarloaf, and the firedogs on which she could roast a tasty piece of meat. Her reputation

as the best cook and housekeeper in Boston had brought paying guests from time to time.

The yoke around Piggy Pig's neck and the ring through her nose bumped the deep trough as she eagerly gobbled the slop. Goody Sherman chuckled, and poured the water into a big tin vat. "Sorry, my fat lovely. But without the yoke to block your way through the gate or the ring to make you easier to catch, you'd be hither and yon. And we'd both be in trouble with the captain."

Ptuuui. Goody spit out her contempt for Captain Robert Keayne. More than once she'd caught his fat thumb on the scale at his store, adding to the weight and price of the items he sold. Mr. High-and-Mighty lived on Lake Shore, with land as far as your eye could measure. Bought by the fines the poor paid to redeem their stray animals, no doubt.

The captain was town crier, shopkeeper, leader of the militia—laughingstock though it was—a deputy in the government, and even keeper of the pound, where stray animals were held. And a pretty penny folks had to pay to get their own animals back, too. It seemed there was nowhere in Boston that the captain's meddling didn't reach.

Goody sniffed indignantly. Why bother herself thinking about the likes of him?

She turned her attention back to her fine pig. Scratching behind the one ragged ear, Goody daydreamed aloud. "Soon there'll be piglets: twelve, maybe even sixteen. With three litters a year, that could be"—she counted on her fingers—"forty-eight piglets. Then we could afford some nice things, we could: some fine cloth from England, a goblet of pewter, or maybe a book." As much as she loved her almanac, it did get tiring reading the same things over and over again. "The captain wouldn't look down his nose at us anymore, no sir."

Goody scowled as she tested Piggy Pig's yoke. "Ummm, it's a mite loose. I'd best tell the mister to fix it."

She hurried home, where potatoes, onions, and carrots bubbled in the pot hanging over the hearth. Using the hem of her skirt as a hot pad, she swung the pot toward her and sniffed deeply. Not bad, considering that it was only clear broth. When there were piglets to trade or sell, things would be better. Goody set the fire shield in front of the fireplace so the heat would bounce back toward the pot. That would hasten the cooking some.

Parrrum, parrrum pum pum. Parrrum, parrrum pum pum. The sound of a snare drum rattled the window as its vibrations rolled across Boston. "Humph," Goody Sherman muttered. That would be the captain and his silly militia of freemen and boys that the richer men could hire to take their places. They were marching up and down, playing soldier.

The king had said the planters needed the militia to defend them against Indians. Yet he wouldn't let them have real guns, for fear they'd someday turn them on him. So the captain and his "army" marched with guns carved from wood. *Parrrum, parrrum pum pum.*

"Durn fool," Goody mumbled. She unlocked the spice box—spices were too precious to leave lying about for the taking—and carefully measured out a variety to enhance the flavor of her soup, sprinkling the spices over the bubbling vegetables. She returned the pot to the fire, then tested the dough she'd left rising on the board. It was ready to form into bread loaves.

The door burst open, and Goodman Richard Sherman pushed through and set down his tool box with a thud. "It's hot enough out there to stew a hen," he complained.

Goody leaned across the board and gave him a quick peck on the cheek. "It's good you're home, Richard. Piggy Pig's yoke is loose, and I'm afraid she'll free herself."

Goodman Sherman pulled their only chair up to the board and sat down. Being the head of the household, he was entitled to sit in a real chair at the board. Like most planters, the Shermans had no real table. Instead they laid a board across wooden horses and put it away when it wasn't in use.

"Now, Elizabeth, you know that pig's too dumb to go through the gate," Goodman Sherman said, laughing heartily. "Besides, I'm not home for good. I just stopped to have a spot of tea and a biscuit to prime my energy."

Goody shot him a stern look as she set down the biscuits. She poured water from the kettle hanging over the fireplace into the teapot with the tea leaves. When the tea had steeped to a proper strength, she strained it into the wooden noggin and scraped a sliver from the sugar-loaf into the tea. Richard liked his tea sweet.

She shoved her trunk to the board and sat down. "Richard, I mean it about the yoke. You should fix Piggy Pig's yoke with no more daw-dling! If she gets away, it will be your—"

"Yes, yes, Elizabeth," Goodman Sherman interrupted. "Later, per-haps. I've still got work for hire to be done."

"Today, Richard!" Goody rammed her fist through the puffy dough, and it collapsed. *Ptuuuuuu.*

Richard winced, as if it were he Goody had just punched. "This evening, then," he said. "I still need to fix the door on Widow Bogg's house. And there's Goodman Peabody's—"

Goody lifted her chin stubbornly. She snatched back the biscuits. "Then you can eat when Piggy Pig is properly yoked!"

Goodman Sherman leaped up, knocking over the chair with a sharp bang. He snatched up his toolbox, then jammed his hat on so hard it bent his ears. "If you aren't the most fire-eating clapperclawer of a wife that ever lived, I'll eat my awl and hammer! You should be hauled straight to the elders for a pond dunking." He stormed out the door with a rush of wind that made the flame in the hearth flicker and jump.

Goody Sherman poked the dough again. Maybe she *was* being overly critical and quarrelsome, as Richard had said. But her pig was like gold in her purse. If anything happened to Piggy Pig, what would she do?

CHAPTER TWO

PIGGY PIG'S
PROBLEM

THE next day was as hot as the day before. The grass had turned brown and brittle underfoot. "I declare, I could fry eggs on yonder rock," Goody Sherman said to herself. She went inside to set her carrot pudding to bake, then gathered her food scraps and hurried to feed the pig. "Sooey," Goody called. "Sooey, Piggy Pig pig pig!"

Goody poured the food into the trough. "Sooey," she called again. "Sooey, Piggy Pig pig pig."

But Piggy Pig didn't come. Then Goody saw Piggy Pig's yoke on the ground. "When Richard gets home this night, he'll get the tongue-lashing of his life!" she promised, shaking her fist toward where she'd last seen her husband.

Parrrum, parrrum pum pum. Parrrum, parrrum pum pum. The snare drum sounded in the distance. "The captain!" Goody gasped. "I'd best be fast in finding Piggy Pig!" Quickly, Goody followed Piggy Pig's hoofprints right to the gate and straight into Widow Hawkes's corn patch. Broken and bent stalks lay half eaten on the ground.

Widow Hawkes stood in the middle of the muddle, her arms folded and her head shaking furiously. "I am fit fer tying," she told Goody. "That corn was fer me and my cow and pig. Now what'll I do?"

"I'll give you corn from my very own garden," Goody promised Widow Hawkes. "But please don't tell the captain."

Widow Hawkes agreed. "I don't hold no good feelings about that old reprobate, and I don't believe in making his job any easier, so I'll gladly keep my silence fer corn. All the same," she said, "if the captain's got her, it's a fat fee you'll pay to get her back."

Goody hurried on toward town, following Piggy Pig's path of destruction. If only she could catch Piggy Pig before the captain did. As she went from door to door, Goody promised each neighbor that she would replace what Piggy Pig had destroyed, if only they wouldn't tell the captain.

Parrrum, parrrum pum pum. The drum got louder as she got closer to town and urged her on.

Goodwife Peabody stood in the middle of her squashed pea patch and offered a mite of pity. "Piggy Pig's probably languishing in Captain Keayne's pound by now," she said. "And I hear the captain's rafting the strays out to summer pasture on Deer Island this very day."

Goody threw her hands up in a helpless gesture, then let them fall to her sides.

Parrrum, parrrum pum pum. The drum rattled the windows and shook the wooden storefronts. The sun beat down on Goody as she stumbled into town and hurried toward the square, where the captain kept the strays. The pen was empty. There was only a notice on the foal gate, growing yellow and brittle in the sun.

All strays are on Deer Island,

a flight-shot from Pullenpoint.

They will be returned

before the harbor freezes over.

Owners may reclaim them then

with the proper payment

of fine and indemnities.

Goody doubled her fists and hit the fence angrily. By now, Piggy Pig was feasting on roots and berries on Deer Island. And the Widow Hawkes was right: it would be a fat fee she'd pay to get her pig back now.

"It's all your fault, Richard!" she yelled at her husband that evening. "If you'd fixed Piggy Pig's yoke when I asked you, she'd still be in her pen. How will we make up the fine?"

"We?" Richard asked. "She's your pig to care for, Elizabeth. She's not worth the price of the fines or the wrath of the captain. He might hire me for work sometime. And I have enough to do now, repairing whatever I can for a modest fee and hunting to bring in a turkey or squirrel now and then."

"Hunting, indeed! Your musket rusts in the corner from disuse." Goody sighed and rested her chin on her fists, brooding. Although they were highly respected hereabouts, she and Richard were poor, the poorest of the poor—even if Richard refused to recognize it. How would she ransom Piggy Pig from the captain? She jutted her chin out stubbornly. "I'll earn the money for the fine through day work. There's carding to do, and I can bake extra bread, and—"

"I'll still want my supper when it's time," Goodman Sherman said. "Forget about that pig and tend to your duties here, Elizabeth. That's my advice to you."

"Pah on your advice, Richard! Supper will be here when you are," Goody promised. "Neither the noggin nor the trencher have gone bare from my lack of doing, and they never will."

"And I want my clothes washed, too," Richard said, ignoring her. "I don't want folks saying that Goodman Richard Sherman's wife doesn't keep him clean."

"They'll be clean as a whistle," Goody promised. "But if you had tended to *your* duties and fixed Piggy Pig's yoke as I said, she'd still be in her pen and suckling a second litter of piglets soon."

"And don't let up on the kitchen garden," Richard warned. "We'll need vegetables and fruit laid up for winter, same as always."

"It'll be done, as always," Goody said. "I will be gardener, cow milker, beekeeper, housekeeper, and cook, as always." But inside she wished it were Richard and not Piggy Pig who was gone.

CHAPTER THREE

PROMISES
TO KEEP

THROUGHOUT the summer Goody toiled in the garden to be sure she had enough vegetables for herself and Richard and for the neighbors whose losses she'd promised to replace. And she baked extra bread, trading that at a bartering stall in town.

Sometimes she'd heave a long sigh and gaze out toward Deer Island, wishing. "How I do long for my Piggy Pig. Why, by the time she returns, she'll have had her piglets, and they'll even be eating on their own. Soon," she would assure herself. "Soon."

Now the leaves on the trees were brushed with gold, and there was a chill in the night air. Autumn had arrived, and Goody counted out her money by the light from the hearth fire. She was still far short of the total she'd have to pay for Piggy Pig's return. She'd have to work faster.

For Goodman Weaver, she carded wool until her fingers were red and raw. For Daniel Maude, the schoolmaster, she washed and ironed clothes, earning sixpence a week. Each coin she earned went straight into her purse until eventually it grew heavy. Surely it would soon be enough to ransom Piggy Pig away from the captain when the raft returned this winter.

Cold winds shook the golden leaves from the trees and fog rolled in from the harbor. "It's as cold as a frog's toes," Goody said. She pulled her shawl closer around her and set thin sticks into the fireplace to make a more brilliant light by which to work.

She sighed gratefully. That was one good thing about this New World—there was enough firewood. Many a night she'd slept cold in England.

In the evenings, Goody worked on her sampler, lest she forget her ABCs and numbers. For the picture, she stitched two likenesses of Piggy Pig, nose to nose. On one she showed the black spot the size of a shilling under Piggy Pig's eye. On the other, she made the ear a bit ragged.

Goody shivered as the hearth fire died down. She glanced toward the loft, where Richard snored peacefully, not giving a fig for Piggy Pig's plight. A fine lot of help he'd been, and it was his fault in the first place that Piggy Pig was gone! Humph!

She yawned and stretched, and climbed the ladder to the loft. Time for some rest before dawn crept through the window and a new day started. There was but one more job to do. Once she'd helped the Wren sisters with their quilts, she'd have enough money to get back Piggy Pig.

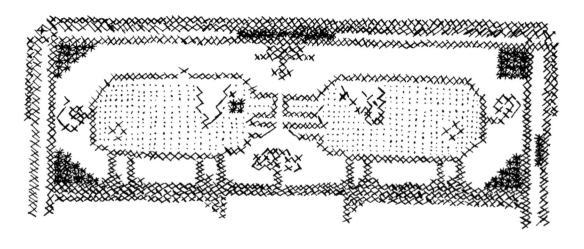

CHAPTER FOUR

COLD WINTER'S
GOSSIP

THE wind blustered in knee-numbing gusts across Massachusetts Bay. Froth-crowned waves leapfrogged over the Boston wharf and slammed into the sailing ships moored there. A mouse-gray fog rolled onto shore and hovered above the rows of houses.

"It's as cold as the captain's charity," Goody told the Wren sisters as she sat across from them, stitching fine, tight stitches on a quilt that stretched nearly the length and width of the room.

They said it was for Agatha's hope chest, although Goody felt sure that Agatha Wren was beyond hope by now. Still, a shilling was not to be sniffed at, so she worked without comment.

Goody looked up from her stitching to gaze through the leaded glass window. Icy rain came down like sharp needles. Already the road to town was so rutted and waterlogged that the men had left their carts in the sheds and put up rope bridges for walking. "Surely the captain will be bringing the animals back from Deer Island soon," Goody said.

"Oh, but they're already back," Agatha said in her twittery voice.

15

"Already back!" Goody said. She would have to reclaim Piggy Pig right away.

"Speaking of the captain, did you hear about the fine feast he gave not a fortnight ago? It was quite a banquet, I hear tell," Agatha added.

"Aye, there was all the gentry in their velvets and brocades and fine laces, with their silver buckles polished to a fare-thee-well. They ate wild rice and turkey, a fine roasted pig, and mince pies topped with cream," Tabitha added.

"Fit for a king, it was," Agatha said, nodding. "A celebration brought on by money he got from overcharging his customers and as keeper of the pound, no doubt."

"No doubt," Goody said. "The animals roam Deer Island, eating only the food that grows there naturally. Yet the captain charges as if he'd grown the food himself! Humph!"

With the last stitch to the quilt, the Wren sisters paid Goody her shilling, and she thanked them kindly and dropped it into her purse.

Goody Sherman pulled her woollen cloak tightly around her and left the Wren cottage. She groaned. "It's so cold a body could spit ice."

Goody shook her purse. It jingled with the coins she'd earned for Piggy Pig's fine. She hurried past the line of houses and down the road a piece, balancing as best she could on the rope bridges over the muddy road. The wind billowed her skirts and set her teeth to chattering. But she was determined to find her pig.

Parrrum, parrrum pum pum. The sound of a snare drum echoed through the streets and rattled the shop windows. *Parrrum, parrrum pum pum.*

It was market day, so the streets were filled with people. A crowd of women and children was gathered near the frog pond, and they pointed their fingers at the ragtag militia and tittered and sniggered and clapped their hands to their mouths.

That fool Robert Keayne had nearly every living, breathing man and older boy in Boston out on the green near the pond. And he, strutting like the peacock that he was, marched ahead of them, shouting his orders above the sound of the drum. *Parrrum, parrrum pum pum.*

Widow Hawkes's son Jethro was beating the drum, and the menfolk were stumble-marching back and forth, smacking one another with their wooden rifles as they turned. *Parrrum, parrrum pum pum.*

The frogs in the pond joined in. *Ribip, ribip, ribeep!* The women and children pointed and tittered, but the men marched on at the captain's command.

"Tree all!" the captain shouted, and every man and boy of them dived to hide behind a tree, tumbling and running into one another in the process.

Goody Sherman shrugged off their silliness. Minding not one bit that she was now ankle-deep in mud, she stomped straight to the pound in the square. She stood on one of the railings of the fence and shaded her eyes to get a better look.

There were sheep and goats and a cow and some pigs milling about in the pound. She saw an all-white pig and an all-black pig and a black-and-white pig and one pig as pink as her very own skin. But Goody Sherman didn't see a fine fat sow with a black spot the size of a shilling under her right eye and one ragged ear. Nor did she see any piglets at all.

Parrrum, parrrum pum pum.

She marched herself out onto the green, stopping the pretend soldiers dead in their tracks. Then she shook a finger right in the captain's

face. "Where is my fine white pig with a black spot the size of a shilling under her right eye and one ragged ear?" she demanded.

The captain's round face turned as red as a cherry, and he yelled to his army, "Dismissed!" He stomped over to the pound in the square and pointed at a black-and-white pig. "There's your pig, Goody Sherman, and it's ten pounds you owe for his upkeep."

Goody Sherman stamped her foot, coming right down on the captain's boot. "My Piggy Pig's no *him,* I'll have you to know. She's a fine white sow with a black spot the size of a shilling under her right eye and with one ragged ear, and I've come to bail her out of your infernal pound."

Captain Keayne's face turned redder than the fire in Goody Sherman's hearth. "Maybe you forgot what she looked like. There's no such pig in the pound."

Then it hit Goody Sherman like a pail of ice-cold water. "That fine feast you had, with wild turkey and rice, glazed carrots, and *roast pig*—you *ate* my pig, you—you—you silly old pilferer!"

C H A P T E R   F I V E

WHERE'S
THE JUSTICE?

GOODY Sherman tapped her foot and glared at the captain. "Well?" she said. "What are you going to do about my pig?"

The captain sputtered and rolled his eyes. "I am Captain Robert Keayne, keeper of the pound, respected shopkeeper, a deputy in the government, friend to Governor John Winthrop. I do not eat stray pigs, Goodwife Sherman!"

"Then where is she—and her piglets?" Goody demanded. "Perhaps *accidentally* mixed in with your own animals?" She didn't believe that for a moment, but thought it best to give him a graceful way out.

"I'll have my Piggy Pig or the worth of her and the three litters of piglets she might have had this year," Goody Sherman promised him. "You can settle with me now, or you can do it in court. After all, what's right is right."

Weeks went by, and the captain made no effort to give Goody her pigs or the money for them. She went to the church elders, as was the custom, and asked for a hearing. The elders agreed to listen to both arguments, and set a date for doing it.

On the day of the hearing, the weavers' looms sat empty, and horses fidgeted unshod outside the blacksmith's shop. The carpenters' hammers lay in their toolboxes. Every man, woman, and child who could wiggle or squeeze into the church crowded in. And those who couldn't waited in the churchyard for word to be passed out to them.

"It's time that come-lately Keayne got his comeuppance," Widow Hawkes whispered. For Captain Keayne hadn't arrived on the *Arbella* with most of the planters. He'd come later, when the tougher work of carving a town out of the wild had been done.

"Goody Sherman is a caterwauling clapperclawer," Jonathan Thatcher muttered. He'd felt Goody's wrath more than once when her roof had leaked after his repairs.

Those who'd been cheated by Keayne and those who'd trembled at Goody's words squabbled among themselves. The Reverend Mr. Cotton, who was running the trial, shushed them all with piously upraised hands. To Captain Keayne he said, "As pound keeper you must advertise found pigs. Did you do this?"

Captain Keayne strutted back and forth like a barnyard rooster as he spoke. The rings on his fat fingers reflected the light from the chandelier. "As keeper of the pound, I nailed a carefully penned notice to my fence. And as town crier, I called the news eloquently through the streets. Many came to look, but none laid claim to her. And she ate more than any ten pigs."

"Ah-ha!" Goody jumped to her feet. She pointed her finger in his face. "You did have a fine white pig with a black spot the size of a shilling under her right eye, and one ragged ear. You admit it!"

The captain sputtered and turned berry red. The crowd muttered among themselves.

"Why didn't you claim your husband's pig?" the Reverend Mr. Cotton asked.

Goody stiffened at the reverend's words. Her husband's pig, indeed! When would women be equals? When would *they* get to own more than the clothes on their backs?

Goody sighed. "First I had to earn the money for the fine."

"There is still a sow in the pound," Captain Keayne said. "Why don't you pay the fine and take her with you now?" Sticking his nose in the air, he added, "And good riddance to bad rubbish, I say."

Goody whirled to face him so fast her skirts slapped against her legs. She stamped her foot. "I saw that sow. That is *not* a fine white pig with a black spot the size of a shilling under her right eye and one ragged ear. It is a scrawny pig that belonged to Goody Gamble. It has no litter in its past and none in its future, is my guess!"

Goody Sherman moved closer to Captain Keayne, until they were nose to nose. Her voice was low and gravelly as she spoke. "A grand host you must have been, serving someone else's pig to your fine friends. That's the same as *stealing!* If you had any conscience at all, you'd have *choked* on it!"

A few of the elders, frequent guests of the captain, rubbed their stomachs uneasily and shifted on the bench.

The crowd tittered, then laughed out loud until the Reverend Mr. Cotton shushed them. "What have you to say for yourself?" he asked the captain.

Captain Keayne touched his mustache as he cleared his throat. He smiled at the elders who sat on the choir bench, waiting to pass judgment, but his face was as red as a soldier's jacket. "I am an *honorable* and godly man."

Goody harrumphed loudly, remembering his fat finger on the scales at his shop. There was a murmur from the crowd, too.

"And a *generous* man," the captain continued, although his face wore a telltale flush. "Had I eaten Goody Sherman's pig, could I now stand before the elders who sit on the very same bench I gave to the church?"

The elders squirmed uneasily.

"And would I now stand bathed in the light of the very chandelier

I gave to the church? Why, if I lied it might fall upon me."

There was a flutter of noise from the spectators as they stepped back a few feet from under the chandelier. The elders buzzed and nodded. Their powdered wigs bobbed while they talked among themselves, then to the Reverend Mr. Cotton.

Finally, the Reverend Mr. Cotton spoke. "Godly men do not eat pigs that are not their own. Captain Keayne is a godly man, or he would not be so generous with the church. Therefore he is innocent."

Captain Keayne's face burst into a wide smile. He shook hands with the reverend and with the elders and with his friends, who Goody was sure had shared roast pig with him.

Goody Sherman wagged her finger at the captain. "You haven't heard the last of this," she promised. "For what's right is right. And it is right that I should have my pig and her piglets or the money they would have brought."

From the back of the church, Goodman Richard Sherman stalked up to Goody. "Don't you know that you can't heat straw to soften it? You must throw water on it."

Goody stamped her foot. "Why couldn't you have stood up here by my side this day? *Now* you come up with advice. If you're suggesting that I throw water on that old billy goat, I'll gladly do it!"

"I only mean that maybe a softer approach would do."

"Oh, pish posh! I want what's mine, Richard, and I'll get it, too!" Goody said.

"Enough, Elizabeth!" Goodman Sherman said. "The men laugh at me in the tavern at night. Everyone is saying I have no control over my wife's blathering."

Goody raised herself to her full height. "It's the truth!" she said.

CHAPTER SIX

NO PIG
IN A POKE

ANOTHER knee-numbing, toe-stinging winter came and went in Boston. And then another. With little else to take their minds off the weather and the hard work to be done, the townspeople continued to argue about the fate of Goody Sherman's pig. And the captain and his ragtag militia still marched near the frog pond. *Parrrum, parrrum pum pum.*

More and more impounded pigs ate and grew fat in the captain's charge. But none of them was white with a black spot the size of a shilling under her right eye, with one ragged ear.

Goody bided her time. The captain was not popular among the people. His luck was running out. Several times he was brought before the elders for cheating his customers. And each time the elders grew less grateful for the bench and the chandelier. Finally, they fined him two hundred pounds and gave him a tongue-lashing he'd not soon forget.

"The captain has even fewer friends than he had before," Goody told Richard. "The time is right to charge the captain again."

"Forget that pig, Goody," Richard warned her. "Maybe the captain was telling the truth. Maybe Piggy Pig died."

"Pah!" Goody said. "There's no truth in the man. Yes, I'll charge him again. Only this time I'll take him before a *real* court, not the church elders." And Goody made her accusations before the inferior court.

Alas, the captain had at least one friend left, for the judge in the inferior court found him innocent of stealing Goody's pig. And the judge made poor Goody pay the cost of the court—three pounds!

The captain was so delighted that he took Goody right back to the same court. "She's telling everyone I stole her pig," he said. "People won't come to my store anymore. That woman is costing me money." The captain dabbed at his eye. "You, wise judge, said I was innocent. So she is calling us *both* liars!"

The judge sputtered, and his face turned red. He glared at Goody. "Both? Liars?" He slammed his gavel on the table. He pointed to Goody. "You must pay twenty pounds," he told her, "for libeling this fine gentleman."

Goody stormed from the court in a real tizzy. That was more money

than she'd see in her lifetime. "It's not fair!" she said. "It should be the captain paying, not me! He's rich, and I'm poor. He's wrong, and I'm right."

The townspeople were angry, too. "They side with the gentry against us poor." The people turned their pockets inside out and their purses upside down. They gathered a shilling here and a halfpenny there. But they could not raise enough to help Goody pay her fine.

Goody paced back and forth. "The General Court meets twice a year. If only I could bring the captain to the General Court," she said. "Many of its members have lodged with us on occasion. Surely they—"

"I am weary of your pig prattle," Goodman Sherman said. "I want no more of it. I'm the laughingstock of Boston, and now there's a fine hanging above our heads. *Your* head, to be exact."

"As men elected by the freemen, the General Court might be more fair," Goody said. She slapped her knee. "If I win there, I'll never have to pay that fine. Somehow I'll do it!"

"Then you'll do it without *me,*" Goodman Sherman said. "The next sailing ship that leaves for England will have me on it, while I still have the money for passage. And I'll not come back until you have gotten that pig out of your head."

Goody sighed. "Then so be it, for what's right is right." Besides, Boston, not England, was her home now, and she was determined to make it a good one. She'd do all right without Richard. There were still neighbors willing to hire her for small jobs. And maybe Richard would send her a little money now and then.

CHAPTER SEVEN

ONE LOST AND
ONE FOUND

GOODMAN Sherman stuffed his tools and his clothes into a trunk and marched himself to the dock where the *Victoria* was moored.

The new ship had brought tea, spices, and a young solicitor named George Story. As Goodman Sherman carried his trunk of tools and clothes up the gangway, George Story carried his box of law books and clothes to the pier.

Goodman Sherman tipped his hat to George Story. "Good day to you, sir," he said in passing.

George Story nodded. "You must be familiar with this fine town," he said. "Tell me if there is room for yet another young, ambitious solicitor."

Goodman Sherman laughed. "My wife alone could give you business enough, so prone to suing is she. That is," he added, "had she the funds with which to pay." He stalked on up the gangway.

George Story called to him. "And what might your wife's name be?" he asked.

"Goodwife Elizabeth Sherman, wife of Richard Sherman," Goodman
Sherman called back. "Our cottage is that way on the main road. But
I'm telling you, there's no money for you there. And it's a stupid suit,
anyway. Goody and her pig are the talk of the town."

George Story laughed. "A pig, you say? The talk of the town? That
might be just what I need to get the attention of the good people." He
thanked Goodman Sherman, then hurried past the rows of look-alike,

whitewashed houses to the house of Goody Sherman.

"So the mister told you of me, did he now?" she said. "And with venom in his voice, I presume. Well, as he probably said, I have no money for a lawyer," Goody told George Story. She gestured around the room. "What you see is mine. This and one cow."

George Story smiled. "What I see is ample, Goodwife Sherman. All I require is a place to bed down at night, light by which to read my books, and victuals on the board. For that I will represent you in court."

Goody eyed him suspiciously. "Why would you practice your bla-blative art on *my* behalf?"

He gestured widely. "For one thing, I'm intrigued by the idea of all this fuss over a pig."

"But a fine pig she was," Goody said, "all white, except for a black spot the size of a shilling, with one ragged ear. And she was giving me three litters of piglets to barter each year. Until that wretched captain and his fancy friends ate her!"

"Goodwife Sherman, I will gladly represent you in court in exchange for lodging and a small share of your food. Word will spread. Paying clients will come."

"Then so be it. You will have room and board in exchange for representing me," she said.

While Goody Sherman worked on her sampler or read her almanac, George Story read his law books. And while Goody slept in her loft, dreaming of a time when she would have another pig, with piglets three times a year, George Story lay on his straw mattress near the fireplace, planning his arguments for court.

It wasn't long before George Story had paying clients, too. Then he paced back and forth, practicing the speeches he'd make on behalf of those few people who'd come to hear of him.

Two more winters passed, and all the while Goody Sherman and George Story went door-to-door, asking neighbors if they remembered Piggy Pig and the year she disappeared.

"I remember a fine fat sow with a black spot under her right eye the size of a shilling, and one ragged ear," Goodman Stokes said. "It was on the raft to Deer Island the very day it was caught by the captain."

"Aye," Goodman Brown said. "And on the raft that returned here that winter, there was a fine fat sow with a black spot under her right eye the size of a shilling and one ragged ear. With a bevy of piglets trailing her, too. Two of them had that same black spot under their right eyes, though the ears were not ragged."

"That would be my Piggy Pig, all right," Goody said. "Piggy Pig and her litter of piglets."

The Widow Hawkes's boy, a young man now, remembered putting a sow of that description and all her piglets into a cart. "Squealing to the heavens, they were," he recalled.

"And where was that cart heading?" George Story asked.

"Why, to the captain's estate on Lake Shore," Jethro Hawkes replied. "The next time I saw those piglets, they were orphans for sure," he added.

Goody doubled her fists and pounded them together. "He served my Piggy Pig to those pompous old men," she said. "And he kept her piglets for his own."

"That's it!" George Story told Goody. "We have enough testimony to take Robert Keayne to court."

CHAPTER EIGHT

ONCE MORE, WITH FEELING

WHEN the captain heard he was to be tried again, he was furious. His friend, Governor John Winthrop, lost his temper, too. "Will we never hear the last of *that woman* and her *pig*?" he shouted.

Of course all the townsfolk knew of the governor's low opinion of women. He had expressed it often enough.

"We will not have an easy time of it," George Story warned Goody. "Just last week I was defending a young woman whose only crime was that she used her mind. Governor Winthrop fined her, saying she'd lost her understanding and reason because she read and wrote books.

" 'She should have kept her place and attended to household affairs and such things as belong to women. She should not meddle in such things as are proper for men, whose minds are stronger,' " George Story quoted the governor.

"Her he accuses of *using* her mind. Me he accuses of *losing* my mind. Stronger minds, indeed!" Goody said. "Pish posh! Stronger of body and weight, perhaps, or sometimes we might thrash them mightily. But *not* of mind. We work as hard as our men in this New World.

And someday we will have as much to say about how it is run, too," she said. "I feel it in my bones."

Goody measured flour into a bowl. Carefully she took a cup from her sourdough stash to add to it. "The governor heads the General Court, and Captain Keayne is not only a good friend of his but also a court deputy. Still, there are others on the court, so surely I will have my justice," she said. She dribbled water into the bowl until the flour stuck together, then kneaded it with her knuckles. "The townspeople will side with a poor woman over that unpopular Captain Keayne. That should have some influence on the deputies, who far outnumber the magistrates."

George Story nodded sympathetically. "Alas, we must deal with the governor and his court as they are, prejudiced and shortsighted on occasion. Yet I feel something good will come of this, Goodwife Sherman."

Goody laid a damp cloth over the dough and set it near the hearth to rise. "If all men, whether or not they owned property, and if all women were allowed to vote, it would be different, I'm sure. Someday . . ."

"Yes," George Story said, "I believe you are right. Someday all men and women will have equal rights. But for now, we'll do our best."

On the appointed day in 1642, Goody Sherman and George Story entered the door beneath the sign of the cod, where the magistrates and deputies met together as the General Court. Again looms sat untended and horses went unshod while the people gathered to see if Goody would win her case at last.

"Good luck," some of them whispered timidly as she and George Story made their way to the front of the big room and sat down.

The magistrates and deputies, dressed in their wigs and robes, entered the room, taking their seats at the front. For seven days they listened to witnesses for Goody and for Captain Keayne.

Jethro Hawkes held up both hands with his fingers spread apart. "The sow I saw had this many and more piglets," he said. "And they all went to the captain's own pens. I saw them with my very eyes."

"Aye," Goodman Brown told the court. "I saw her myself—a fine fat sow with a black spot under her right eye the size of a shilling and one ragged ear, with a bevy of piglets trailing her. She was taken straight off the raft to the captain's personal pens."

But for every witness George Story brought to the stand, Robert Keayne brought ten more who said they had seen no such pig. Mrs. Keayne, in her finest of frocks, took the stand. "The woman accuses us falsely," she said. "We have many fine pigs. We have no need of someone else's. Besides, she denied ownership of the stray we kept. The woman doesn't know her own pig."

Whispers hissed and buzzed in the courtroom as the crowd commented on each witness. Again and again, Governor Winthrop banged his gavel and called for order.

Goody stirred in her seat. How could the captain's family stand up there and defend him like that, claiming they had not taken Piggy Pig? Still, she could tell from the murmurings of the crowd that they were on her side. Surely that would influence the deputies and magistrates, who, after all, had to walk among them once this was over.

The deputies and the magistrates argued loudly and angrily. And when they were finished, fifteen deputies voted for Goody Sherman. Eight voted for the captain.

Of the magistrates, seven voted for the captain. Only Mr. Bellingham and Mr. Saltonstall voted for Goody. Seven members of the court couldn't make up their minds, so they didn't vote at all.

Goody counted on her fingers. Seventeen votes for her. And only fifteen votes for the captain. "We have two more votes than the captain," she told George Story. "We win! We win!"

CHAPTER NINE

GOODY'S
REVENGE

GOODY Sherman did a little jig and clapped her hands. At last she would have her justice.

"The nays have it," the governor said, banging his gavel.

Angry hisses and boos erupted from the crowd. Goody stopped her jig and cried out, "No! This can't be!"

Those who'd voted in Goody's favor stood, shaking their fists angrily, demanding a recount of the vote.

"I'm sorry," George Story told Goody. "But a majority of the magistrates voted no. And the governor is letting the negative vote stand. A majority of both bodies must agree."

"Where is the justice in this?" Goody demanded.

George Story shrugged. "It is the law."

"It's not fair!" some of the people shouted. "Where is the justice for a poor woman?"

Governor Winthrop looked pleased. But the members of the court were still shouting at him, demanding that the statute permitting the negative vote be removed.

"No!" one of the magistrates who'd voted for the captain shouted. "If the majority of both parties ruled, the deputies, by your sheer numbers, would always outvote the magistrates. The statute must stand."

Governor Winthrop scowled at the bickering men. He said, "Those who gave witness *against* the captain hold some prejudices against him and gave evidence only of probability. Those who gave witness *for* the captain gave certain evidence upon their own knowledge. Those who voted against the captain allowed their judgments to blind them against the true nature and course of the evidence before them. Therefore, the negative vote by those clearheaded court members prevails and demonstrates the goodness of the negative vote."

He pointed to Mr. Bellingham and Mr. Saltonstall, the two magistrates who'd voted in Goody's favor. "Change your vote," he urged them. "Let us make the vote of the magistrates unanimous."

"Yes!" shouted the other magistrates.

Finally, Mr. Saltonstall changed his vote and was mightily booed for it.

Angrily, Mr. Bellingham refused, denying Governor Winthrop his unanimous vote. "Furthermore, I shall write a paper telling of the evils of the negative vote!" he promised.

"Do!" some of the deputies shouted. "Write it!"

The deputies and the magistrates raised their voices at one another in fury, although they were very nearly drowned out by the spectators.

Goody stormed from the room, leaving them to bicker among themselves. In despair, Governor Winthrop threw his hands up in surrender. "At least we must show the people of Boston that we can agree on *something* before we leave," he said. "Let us vote that we all have great admiration and charity for one another. All those in favor say 'aye.' "

The deputies and the magistrates sat in stubborn silence, their arms folded defiantly across their chests. There was not an aye among them.

Grimly, Governor Winthrop called for the nays. The room echoed with loud nays. The men *did* agree on something at last. They agreed that they did *not* have great admiration and charity for one another.

This was followed by bickering and name calling as everyone took one side or the other for what seemed like hours. But suddenly there was even more noise! All kinds of pigs—pink ones, black ones, black-and-white ones, and two with black spots the size of shillings under their right eyes—came snuffling and snorting down the aisle. And behind them was Goody Sherman, stick in hand, yelling at the top of her voice, "Sooey, piggies! Sooey!"

Ronk ronk wheeeee wheeeeee. The pigs raced down the aisle, sending people scurrying to stand on top of the benches.

"See," Goody shouted. "Right here among the captain's own pigs are two that are surely the descendants of my Piggy Pig."

Captain Keayne, doing his best not to be trampled by the unruly pigs, mopped his face with a handkerchief. "Goodwife Sherman, if I withdraw my judgment of twenty pounds against you, will you return these infernal pigs to my pen and leave me alone?"

"No," Goody replied, slapping the floor with the stick and causing pigs to scatter in all directions.

"If I give you back the three pounds in court costs, as well?"

"No."

"Robert!" Governor Winthrop shouted. "Do something! Do anything! Only get that woman from my sight!"

Ronk ronk wheeeee wheeeeee.

"Take the two with spots under their eyes!" Captain Keayne yelled when one of the pigs pulled at his silver shoe buckle.

The pigs grunted and squealed as the younger, more athletic boys of Boston dived and grabbed at them, driving them into a corner of the courtroom. With her stick, Goody deftly separated her two piglets, who were the image of her own Piggy Pig, and drove them to the courtroom door.

She turned toward the captain and the governor. "There is just one more thing."

"What?" both men shouted at once.

"Governor Winthrop called good people prejudiced and blinded to justice."

Governor Winthrop nodded. "That was not sufficient warrant for me

to break out into any distemper. I did arrogate too much judgment of religion and reason to myself and too little to others. I will write a paper of apology in the cause of peace."

Goody nodded with satisfaction and poked the pigs with her stick, urging them through the door.

"Good riddance to bad rubbish," the captain shouted at her back. "At least you can't sue me again."

Goody smiled wryly over her shoulder while she ushered her new pigs down the steps. "Don't count on it," she said. Then she left with a flurry, leaving the other pigs to be driven by the young boys to the captain's pen.

"We should take down the cod sign and put up a pig!" one of the magistrates grumbled.

GOODY Sherman took good care of her new pigs, and they brought her so many litters that she was able to live comfortably.

Even though Goody Sherman was at last satisfied, the arguments among the people and the deputies and magistrates continued to rage as the people tried to understand this new system of government, in which only nine men had the power to override a yes vote by more than twice their number.

Despite Governor Winthrop's argument that reading and writing should be taught at home, Deer Island was taken from the captain that very same year and turned over to the schoolmaster for a free school for the young boys in the township. And eventually the governor wrote his public apology to those members of the court who had voted for Goody and to her witnesses. His paper was copied and passed among them to read, as was the custom.

Most of the magistrates and the deputies forgot about Goody Sherman. But they continued to fight with one another.

"If we sit side by side in the same room, and we vote together, why are our votes counted separately?" a deputy argued. "We are thirty people and the magistrates are but nine, yet their negative voice can discount our yes votes."

"It is too hard for the common people to understand this if we sit together," one deputy said. "I don't understand it myself! I think we should sit apart, in different houses. That way it will be easier to understand."

"Sitting apart may make it easier to understand," another argued. "But it won't help us. Only the magistrates are empowered to make laws. What if they decide to do away with our body altogether?"

The magistrates understood that the deputies and the commonfolk wanted a system they believed to be fairer. So it was that another change took place. Two years after Goody Sherman lost her last court battle and seven years after she had first accused the captain of stealing her pig, the deputies and the magistrates agreed that they would never again meet under the same roof or vote together. From that day forward, they would meet and vote in separate houses. But at last the deputies were given the power to create laws, provided that a majority of the magistrates voted in their favor. And they were given the power to reject a law proposed by the magistrates, if a majority of the deputies voted nay. Despite the difference in their numbers, both bodies were now equal in status.

More than one hundred years later, long after Goody Sherman and her pig had been forgotten, the founding fathers of the United States designed a new government using the divided houses that the colonies had used, instead of the parliamentary system that England still used. They called their two bodies of government the House of Representatives and the Senate.

Perhaps they didn't remember how the new system had come into being. But Governor Winthrop could have told them. "It was Goody Sherman's pig that did it!"

DATE DUE			
DEC. 2 1995			

F 8
Chr   Christian, Mary Blount.
        Goody Sherman's pig

GAYLORD M2